Back to School, Picky Little WITCH!

Back to School, Picky Little WITCH!

By Elizabeth Brokamp
Illustrated by Peter J. Welling

PELICAN PUBLISHING COMPANY

GRETNA 2014

To Darlene. And thanks to Shawn, Justin, Michael,
Andy, Mary, Heather, Missy, Christina, Kasen, Kara, Jacy,
David, and Matthew for keeping me young at heart.—P. J. W.

Library of Congress Cataloging-in-Publication Data

Brokamp, Elizabeth.
  Back to school, Picky Little Witch! / by Elizabeth Brokamp ; illustrated by Peter J. Welling.
     pages cm
  Summary: "It's back to school for the Picky Little Witch. She'll need a jar of red newts' eyes,
boxes of toads for spell practice, and a black cauldron. But when she and Mama Witch head for
Witches R Us, the battles begin over which items Mama recommends and which items the Picky
Little Witch really wants"—Provided by publisher.
  ISBN 978-1-4556-1887-3 (hardcover : alk. paper)—ISBN 978-1-4556-1888-0 (e-book)
  [1. Witches--Fiction. 2. Witches—Fiction. 3. Shopping—Fiction. 4. Compromise (Ethics)—
Fiction. 5. First day of school—Fiction.] I. Welling, Peter J., illustrator. II. Title.
  PZ7.B7863Bac 2014
  [E]—dc23

                          2013033298

The illustrations in this book were inspired by characters created by Marsha Riti.

Printed in Malaysia
Published by Pelican Publishing Company, Inc.
1000 Burmaster Street, Gretna, Louisiana 70053

BACK TO SCHOOL, PICKY LITTLE WITCH!

"Witch mail for you!" Mama Witch sang out, handing the Picky Little Witch a fancy black envelope.

"Oh, goody!" the Picky Little Witch said, clapping her hands. "I love getting witch mail." She opened the letter and read it out loud.

"Calling little witches, ghosts, and ghouls!
Back to all your scary schools.

On the first day, bring these supplies,
including a jar of red newts' eyes.

You'll also learn the name of your teacher
(hopefully, a scary creature).

We'll see you at the start of September
for a frightening year we'll all remember!"

The Picky Little Witch stopped reading and showed Mama the list of school supplies.

witches school

- School supplies for little witches.

1   Cape
1   Hat
2   Pairs of boots
1   Broom
1   Jar of red newts' eyes
1   Bottle of bacterial soap
2   Boxes of toads for spell practice
1   Medium sized black cauldron
1   Cat

Mama Witch sighed. "I'll go start the broom. It looks like we have some shopping to do!"

The Picky Little Witch and her mama boarded the broom and headed for Witches R Us, the spookiest department store in town.

"I love this place," the Picky Little Witch said, eyeing a "Back to Ghoul" display. "Here's the list, Mama. What shall we look for first?"

Mama Witch held up a little black cape with strings that tied at the neck. "Ooooh, this is nice. How about this one?"

"A black cape that's dark as night
is sure to give anyone a fright.

The scratchy fabric is so nice and sturdy,
plus no one will know if you get dirty!"

"Too plain," said the Picky Little Witch.

"Okay. Moving along to shoes then." Mama held up a
pair of black boots.

"Look over here. How about these?
Perfectly pointy, certain to please.

BOOTS

OTS

B

BOOTS

BOO-Ts

BOOTS

BOOTS

B

With a hundred buttons to fasten just so,
in shiny black leather from tip to toe.

Go ahead," she urged. "Try them on."

The Picky Little Witch took a boot from Mama's outstretched hand and tried to slip it on her foot.

"Ouch," she said. "Definitely too tight."

Mama Witch sighed. "We'll have more luck with a broom, I think." She picked up one of the plain straw brooms.

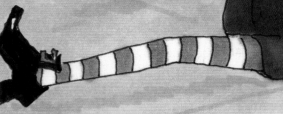

"How about this one, of heart of pine?
Standard straw bristles and straight as a line.

No need for the fancy fiberglass stick
when old-fashioned wood will do the trick."

"But I might get splinters," the Picky Little Witch
said. "I definitely don't want splinters."

"You can't be worried about splinters if you're going to grow up to be mean and scary," Mama Witch said.

The Picky Little Witch shook her head stubbornly.

"Can I help you?" asked the saleslady.

"Not unless you have a potion that makes little witches more reasonable," Mama Witch grumbled.

The saleslady smiled sympathetically. "No such luck," she said, "but I may have something else. I'll be right back." She hurried away and across the store.

Mama Witch turned to the Picky Little Witch. "My dear Little Witch, what do you like?" she asked, exasperated.

"That all black thing is kind of . . . um . . . " The Picky Little Witch paused, looking at the capes.

"Go on," prodded her mother.
"Well, it's dreary, dark, old, and glum.

A rainbow-colored cape is best
with fleecy lining and sequined vest."

Then the Picky Little Witch pointed at a traditional witch hat and wrinkled her nose.

"And no modern little witch wants a pointy hat.
This is so much better than that."

"That's your favorite? A green beret?" her mother asked.

"It's even topped with a big fluffy feather!
So I'll be in style no matter the weather," the Picky Little Witch added cheerfully.

"No buttons on my boots, pretty please-y.
The new kind have Velcro, quick and easy,

and round is the new pointy when it comes to toes.
My feet won't end up squashed in those."

She paused and looked over at the broom display.
"The wooden broom is so passé—
not suitable for witches of today.

The modern witch wants something comfy and fast,
not like the toothpicks of the past."

"Like this one,"

she said, pointing at a glittering silver broom with a built-in seat made of downy purple fluff and a motor-pack attached to the back.

Mama Witch had heard enough.

"It's true the old brooms are plain and dull,
but they're perfect for when the moon is full.

And as for a beret, not a pointed hat,
this says 'witch' far better than that.

What's next? A pet monkey instead of a . . ."

"Kittens!" the Picky Little Witch cried.

"I was going to say 'cat,'" Mama Witch replied grumpily.

"No, Mama. Look! Kittens!" the Picky Little Witch exclaimed again.

The saleslady headed over, a large wicker basket in her arms. "I may have something you'll like," she said, gesturing for them to come closer.

BATS
VATS
HATS
CATS
RATS

The Picky Little Witch ran over and beckoned to her mother. "Mama, come see!"

Mama Witch peered into the basket just in time to see a little black cat give a big yawn. A little white cat with black paws caught sight of its own tail and began to bat at it.

"Oh, look how cute he is," the Picky Little Witch said. "I love him."

"He's definitely cute. Look at all that beautiful black fur."

"I was talking about the white one," the Picky Little Witch said.

She and her mama stopped and looked at one another, then back at the kittens.

They burst into

laughter.

"You know, they're both really cute," Mama Witch said.

"They are," the Picky Little Witch agreed.

"And you know, there is a cat on your school-supply list."

They smiled at one another, then turned to the saleslady.

"We'll take them," they chorused.

"I thought you might," the saleslady said. "I'll go ring you up. Will that be all today?"

"Not yet, I'm afraid," Mama said. "For one thing, we still need boots." She bent down to struggle with her own boot. "I always did hate all those buttons.

Putting my boots on took forever.
Velcro does seem much more clever."

The Picky Little Witch quickly selected a shiny pair
of button-less boots.

"As for capes, the rainbow one is pretty but bright,
and not really made for creatures of the night.

A basic black cape will help you hide
and let the moonlight be your guide."

"But—" the Picky Little Witch protested.

"No arguing or we'll head home now,
quicker than you can say . . ."

"Meow!" one of the kittens called out. The Picky
Little Witch giggled.

"Exactly," Mama Witch said, smiling.

"As for a hat,
let me think about that."

WITCHES
R
US

She sighed. "I guess a beret would be okay.

But black, please, for witch's sake.
There's only so much change a mama can take!"

The Picky Little Witch clapped her hands. "Yay!

Could I get a cushy broom with a little zing?
Sparkles would be just the thing."

"Splinters are definitely overrated," Mama Witch said cheerfully.

"A cushioned seat will do the trick
but only on top of an old-fashioned stick.

If you work hard this year and pass each test,
we'll add some glitter and some zest."
"Thank you, Mama. You're the best!"

MINI BROOM CUSHIONS

SALE

SALE

The saleslady handed Mama Witch a great big bag and gave the basket with the kittens to the Picky Little Witch. "Here, young lady."

"Thank you. Thank you, too, Mama. I love you."

"You're welcome, my Picky Little Witch. I love you, too."

Mama Witch and the Picky Little Witch headed home, happy that they could agree on the most important thing of all.